FANNY HAWKE GOES TO THE MAINLAND
FOREVER

FANNY HAWKE GOES TO THE MAINLAND FOREVER

Sebastian Barry

Raven Arts Press/Dublin

Fanny Hawke Goes to the Mainland Forever
is first published in 1989 by
The Raven Arts Press
P.O. Box 1430
Finglas
Dublin 11
Ireland.

ISBN 1 85186 060 6 (softback)
ISBN 1 85186 071 1 (hardback)

Raven Arts Press receives financial assistance from the Arts Council (An Chomhairle Ealaíon), Dublin, Ireland.

Cover design by Susanne Linde. Design by Dermot Bolger & Aidan Murphy. Printed in Ireland by Future Print Ltd., Baldoyle.

CONTENTS

ACKNOWLEDGEMENTS

Grateful acknowledgements are made to the editors of the following papers and journals, where these poems were first printed:

Antaeus (New York), Krino (Galway), The Iowa Review, New Irish Writing (The Irish Press), The Irish Times, Ironwood (Tucson), London Magazine, London Review of Books, Poetry Ireland Review, Poetry Wales, Rubicon (Montreal), The Salmon (Galway), Stand Magazine.

for Alison

LITTLE ITHACA

Yes, I have walked through a plethora of old
cultured cities, whether mould or masonry,
whore or heraldry, and on my way what I saw
were the insides of small rooms, stationfuls
of hawkers going somewhere, rooms like mine,
lights gratefully sleeping on the rivers
allowing momentary respite to the watchers,
lovers, loners, plain-clothes thieves and such.
I did not get talking to any of them,
I was up in the golden library scribbling
to keep myself warm, the scent hot

and few things were as fast as the rush
of recognition when the words settled
on my pages, ducks twisting their heads to sleep
on a greensward, and I looked up and hoped
again — that this foreign place might be the vessel
of lamplight and sun's grace, of grass
that would pillow my form in easiness
when I was tired of walking on the cinders
of paths of public parks that celebrated
victories even my grandparents never prayed for.
And this I did for so many years,

perfecting the melancholy of the wanderer,
leading myself into a grave impasse,
singing less, singing less, singing less.
And now I have lived with you a summer
and other unsuspected unknown seasons
and I come like a poor respectful friend
of gentling Catullus to the pretty pass
of praising your local colour in my own city
that I abandoned as ordinary, ordinary.
But you have made by grace of extended welcome
my home extraordinary, extraordinary, truly.

THE ONLY TRUE HISTORY OF LIZZY FINN, BY HERSELF

Starchy cheering burghers of Brighton or Bexhill,
the wintry theatres, clay pipes, wood pipes, Havana
   puffs,
the roof-fulls of cherubs, brown seaside streets,
my hair with its weights, black bloom, grey bloom.
Then Robert Gibson took me off through the lamp-adoring
Welsh farms, and in the empty stomach of the packet-
   steamer
he smudged my sharp rouge. The inky sea with furious
   fishes
was under us, and on his back lay my long white arms
and over us the passengers walked the scrubbed decks
in the night-time, with a big bruised sky, a crushed
   moon.

I found a world of tobaccos, billiard-tables, calicoes,
giggles between stepping-stones like children's buckets,
shires with fetlocks as shaggy as my stage drawers,
a marriage in Christ Church, the lonely vicars,
lost sparrows in the blueness under the shooting vault,
pressed collars ranked against me at a spanking table,
strolls in sober rain to see the romantic ruins
and Lady Gibson despairing about the jam stains
marking my Sunday linens, and Robert heaving
forever like a sailor on the rope of my drifting.

We had a daughter, a pretty red-skinned daughter
fit to burst her swaddling-clothes, grubby as me.
I joyed to crush her till she wept in my lap
and I tossed her into the sombre slaty skies
when the mower-man showered the granite-chip paths
and that tang of cut grass got into my dreams.
There was everything to do, the cooks to content,
my a's to say long, the box of brimming needle-work
that I couldn't finish fast enough to fit the child.
Her legs shot down, arms out, the stable-clock rattled.

At night I went up to the old house tower.
It was full of the true histories of spiders,
trophies from a war that had clipped a hedge of sons,
stray bits of lawn-sports still saying thwack and pock.
The moon kept it as her house and below me
the slow ratchets of the mansion loosened and whirred.
There in the best light, with my candle shadows,
I hitched my Belfast linens, English and Indian silks,
and showed my starry crotch to the stiff-backed toys
and danced for all ye who carry my whoring pride.

THE TIDE HOTEL

The seventeenth century as modern as the netted dawn.
Small chalk, like animals, against the lighthouse,
the maker of powder cones,
a cigar in the skipper's eyes.
He lures the shore to his rowing-boat, a basket.
His soft ship at his back
a cloud caught in a tree.

On the morning quay an artist strokes it down.
His lead is light. The pair of passengers
shivers inside satin,
their lice woken by the breeze,
it is half summer.
The shock-feigning faces
work the oarsmen to the wall.

The artist ignores them as familiar,
anchors the vessel soundly on his paper
and shifts his bottom to let go zephyrs
of sausages and black bread.
The first dress imports saffron up the steps,
offending him,
and stops like a moon on the stone planks.

His bloodied cat comes to him with a loosened rat.
The second dress shakes itself over small pale boots,
grows gorgeously.
The artist notes the ship has swung
and spoiled his aim
as the tide turns back to town.
The ordinary flowers hurry to the granite hotel.

MARY DONNELAN, SEAMSTRESS OF THE MAD

Mary, the half-cocked shadow under the awning
of the locked butcher's is just a bin of rabbits
  gone bad
not the very incarnation of a novelette villain,
sweet tooth, sharp nail, deceptive smile and all.
So press on with your linen layers gripped by one
  paw
out of the mere appearances of the dawn street
in under the arch of the Sligo Lunatic Asylum,
leaving the moon to glister at the waking women
of the whole town, stirring in their caves to break
the fresh ice on the liquid slugging in the
  washing-jugs.
Here in the brown halls of a world apart, the moon's
own men are dreaming in one half of sugar and spice,
the moon's good women in the other of slugs and snails.

As you pick your way to the sewing-room, remember the
  similar
barracks in Athlone, where the red cloths of the uniforms
were plaques of middle-burning coals on the dark walls
and your father, Gibson's batman, was not your father,
your mother not your mother, and you made your own
  story
like any other orphan or farmed-out child, and the big bells
tolled every other story in symbol from the old
  cathedral
and, daughter of grace or disgrace, you learned to sew
so that sofas and armchairs even could have family
histories, decked as icons and pictorial panels on their
  backs.
Mary, in the hours coloured purple and blackly baked

17

of that previous country, walk in in your second-best
   bonnet
with a flourish of pheasant feather, and take your
   needle
off the work-desk grained with dawnlight from the
   grubby
lattices, and apparel Sligo's mad in astute designs
because they are the creatures in the keepers' dominion
who can't lift a hand outside their dreams, sleeping
or waking. Work in the dark to put them in a good light
of dresses, for instance, to make the captain's wife
   jealous
with sure pleating and ribbing and shoulders smeared
   with gold
or otherwise they'll wander in the cambered corridors
   and close
yards with their arms hitched like yard-arms. Mary,
with charity cloth beyond all redemption, redeem them.

RUDIMENTS OF TAILORING

The neon of the shopsign
carried into the stouty
passage on the brackets

my ears are (it felt like):
*Moran's Bar and Meeting
Rooms,* Kenmare. A measure

cooled in my paw,
the chamber disappearing
under wins. The widows

caused a quiet ruckus
with their nails, cupping
the losing cards, the bulb

stealing a glance
at the polished Jacks
and Queens, and dark

linoleum. A rustle
of chairlegs at our jokes.
Gloom gathering

in the ball of malt,
last of the night,
till everything spun

there: young-days, Mick
Collins, toothpaste.
The blank of a strange

home. All change! The old
man's harbour in the morning.
The very memory

of the stairs gone west
like the carriage
in the Marx Brothers

feeding the fire
in the flea-pit at
Killarney. Josey waiting

in string-vest and dotage
with nothing to say
for himself, and less for me.

Cockcrow disturbing
every last leaf
on the laurel the old man

seeded by mistake,
in the dripping
outside the door. I know

the cock that crows.
Away by the murky whins
the sighing of our horse,

the friend who ploughs
(I shoe him cold), and
the nonsense of the crows.

The ewes skittish
with the men of light
(the shadows that wake up

in the hawthorns
like shepherds, smoking
with astonishing berries)

in the kettle of another
sun. Government pines
marching with sappy

pikes and axes
against a dun on old
ground. A pattern-book

of hours, a guarantee
of slumber and Aspro.
Jesus it would have me

speechless, the yellow
whiskey and the
brother-warm bed. Reduced

to the city traffic
of the robins and the rooks
clashing over

a small matter of grain,
the rooks winning
by dint of heavyweight

(what year was it
Jack Dempsey got away?)
O Christ protect me.

THE LIGHT BRIGADE
for Miko Russell, who tuned it at Clifden

Six hundred shadows
driven from their farms
by a hap of the harvest

onto hazel-haggard lanes,
leaving whin-stubbing,
mud-turfing and gleaning,

cattled to Louisburgh,
a river town without trout.
Their hunger in a herd

inquired after visions
of sudden fodder
or a docket to the workhouse

all else failing
from the Officer of Relief:
"I have no means

to offer you food.
And your ticket machine
is gone to Westport

to stamp bills for the play.
Apply to Colonel Hograve
and Mr Lecky. I pay them

to hear such echoes."
Six hundred backs
unembarrassingly bare

felt a breeze to their candle,
stomachs with child
astray on children.

Under signs, like rags
they murmured to a doze
where a third stiffened

and couldn't be trees.
Gravel and sunrise
raised them like chalices,

the grace of their hunger
to clouds crossed with silver.
Printing like wolves,

as mysterious and as bountied,
a sough in their silence,
they crept against their journey.

A stream at Glankeen
had eaten the rain,
a vein to the grateful bog.

It had little in its gift,
no vicarage of manners:
where water painted

the cold strove to weave.
On the second bank
the hours started over:

their stare couldn't read
any road or shoofly
between nowhere and Doo.

They chose a goats' macadam
up the cliff without ocean
that devalues the asking

on the house Houstan owned.
A torrent with a voice
had no bridge to snout:

they muddled through its horns.
At Delphi Lodge
in Bundorragha

the Guardians were at lunch,
could not be disturbed.
The pines felt an autumn

drift to their roots:
some of that leaf-fall melted.
When the gentlemen

had looked to their digestion
they gave the farmers
the favour of an audience:

"We are not Christ among his people.
Our scones do not multiply,
our salmon are true fish.

The burdens of Empire are many:
you are only one riddle.
Gospel vindicates us.

Go about your business."
They turned from the smell
to the sanctuary of their lodge.

"Gentlemen, embered in empire,
linen and disdain,"
starts rhetoric after the rain.

Sunset tossed a coat
on the ten-mile stumble back.
They smudged past Houstan's home,

its windows dead with stars,
and bargained with the flood.
Ironed by the instrument

they stubbled and looked
or flew too close to the moon,
cluttering off the cliff

like woodlice blown by skirts.
These limbs the lake made secret.
Low numbers and knaves

moistened at Glankeen.
Woken at noon,
the Relieving Officer

shooed gaggles to the trail
who coffined the armfuls
in shallow earth

and where there was none
scooped the farmers
and flapped them to the glen

and pitted them at intervals
as if some question
had been settled between equals

and this was mole-work
after battle:
stupid Paddy burying bloody peasant.

Note: This poem is indebted to Death At Doo Lough
from Tales of the West of Ireland by James Berry.

KELSHA YARD, 1959

i

The ordinary door waiting
for the tree's shadow
to go in without a blessing
at six or seven
lies open to the horse's breathing
that stirs the painted yard.
One hen eats the seed of all
at speed of colour
under the unaccustomed hedges.

ii

Sara's legs a museum of thigh-bones,
pillars in some small-town courthouse style
declaring peace against Annie's hens,
sabre-rattling with sabres of foggy grain,
"Go back, go back, go back."

iii

Ice-queen with crab-apples
left alone among spiders and lichen
and fallen in her cheeks,
Annie looms, a bittern,
in the ice-cream colours
of the dairy, doing
what every day will do
to every milk, box the strange
butter. On moonish enamel
under her mooned nails,
the yellow turf like
paper packages, deep and buttercup,
its creases patted on
by tiny oars.

iv

This horse is a ruinous man
who threw them out
at some clench of byway
in his hurry for hay.
He'll swell now in a browning byre,
a stove of oats,
till the door won't let him go
into the shafts of varnish and foggy lamps
on Sundays and rain days.

v

The dump is fuller than a river,
all the clock its fueller.
Carrots have died white deaths in here,
old turnips make a bad living,
flies start the universe of flies
from time to time,
describe themselves to hens,
tell rotten jokes.
In the middle a boy's
fire-engine flashes,
scattering crimsons
at the stopped roots,
travelling urgently.

vi

The best hen
like a failed ballet dancer
in a rusty tutu
taking liberties and bows forever,
rushes to the boy's shadow.
He springs a dead bucket on her.
In the lacy rays the hen shifts from fork to fork
a grainless week,
telling itself the same story over and over
till its eyes are stars.

vii

Outlandish in smell,
shaking blood
at their own strange speed
onto the loaves of granite,
the gipsy voices of geraniums,
summer's conscience on the sills.

viii

In the deep of breathy strawlight
the old noses of stupid calves
behind iron rails and nails.

ix

Annie's hand like a calf's lips
the sadly cow must think.
Mother-of-pearl drops
smelling of inside skin
hosed over the boy's slowness
from the first hose,
the cow's electric cable.
Annie's features staunchly
long with a skinny laugh
in the huff of shadow,
making the solid pearls
shatter like milk
on the world of hays
and melt
on his clay cardigan.

X

Random as flowers fashioning,
bringing rural emblems like holy medals
in their winter-coats of hair,
September's tinkers moult on the scrabble of cobbles,
metalling the late-afternoon musts and sunken dews
with curse words like luck-money,
laying down threats against famous gifts
of soda and flour,
the sums of bread
on the edge of Rathdangan
under the waterfalls of all places' end,
the pines stockinged in sewing-needles,
the rabbit-man stepping out from the hoaxing scrub
with his stick of dangling snags.

xi

The field-brim lumbered with scrub-oaks,
wet-witted men, a meagre shade
with a thickening for dark suits beyond
embracing or greeting in a shifting gorse.

xii

In dizzy elms
their smudge of cottage,
tea-black as turf.
Someone crosses the grass with a bucket of mice,
a chimney-fire of hair, polka-dotted smock,
to a black sinking cow
in the shelter of its bones
whose milk is always pink,
its snaily nostrils down
making the herringbone clouds
in the clovers moist and humped as moles.

xiii

Annie's purse a hardlived toad
that she gives him to carry
on the green road,
the crust varnishing after a cup of rain.
Faced by the fun of the bellflowers
that sit pretty on a cushy bank
and want their smallest bags
to be thumbed and crimsoned
with a puffing pop among the woken moths
and a palmful of perfume briefer than the blackbird
    resting,
the old purse with silver coins inside like knuckles
makes a toadleap from his care
into the Australia of the ditch.
It hardens her
for the ever of half the road.
At the gate she laughs like a sheepdog,
"Wher, wher, wher."

xiv

Out of strawy boxes
seventy years before
these plates sunned softly,
a sequence of admired dawns,
false tongues on them from the fire,
dawning now deftly under
the kitchenroof carrying the coughing owls
but over the sable boatmen in the bucket.

XV

His sister locks the world's door,
makes her legs an alley
smoking minutely with oranges,
beckons him in.

xvi

The moon a ripe head
in a well of cloud-gap
icy and weedy.
The flustered storm above
stirring nothing below,
the elms as silent
as the graves of sheepdogs
where Sara greens her knees.
The cloud scraping,
a surfeit of granite,
over the moon's drinking-water
with a tiny clank.

xvii

The pad of a marauder becoming
a hedgehog's stillness
in the next world of her lamp
where the windfall mulberries
which dropped in a lull
become less real than it,
purple stones at its feet
in juicy dark,
her splashing yellow
jumpy in the yard
as she angles at the rustling door
in choring candlelight.

xviii

Every real night,
candles no longer coaxed out of warm wax bags,
Sara settles in her own illume,
a murmur of pink perm,
her bedroom as shipshape as a ship.
Over the unmapped badlands of her form,
a bush on each eye,
the sun of her interest loosens like a hound
with a country shadow like a wedding-blanket
as he and Annie survey her from the door.
Out of her own night a prayer breaks,
a blur of moorhens,
but strangely
not in her voice but his
and Annie winks
to make him normal.
The words go
like a wasp inside a jar,
"Alone, alone, alone."

xix

Annie cuts roads for herself
with the poker in the heavy-eyed ashes,
forgetting him
caught in the hedgegap of two imagined fields.
He goes to nest with his sister.

XX

They stand, boy and great aunt, maybe hoping
it all may stand,
maybe forgetting to,
peering over the secrets of nowhere
in the harbour of a hawthorn.
It is still, like a rain-barrel.
The heather is on a famous voyage like a storm.
The things themselves are
in a fleshly camera,
his head a hooded box
in dull sunshine,
he a detail in her days
whose hand she holds.
They have found the scoop of drink
muddied before them
by another's bucket,
the nest of water
with a dirtied bird.
The scum known,
all nightmare overcome
with eggs and flanks
and tending of ashes.
Their bucket, zinc and tinker,
creaks in her free hooks
as they wait for the phoenix to settle.

THE LIFE BY BURNING OF BRIDGET CLEARY

It is weeks of filthy rain. Up on the thistly thatch
showers thicken the newer stalks, and the deep straw, black
from a history of such weathers, shifts on the bony
    rafters
and our cabin walks closer to the lake. The swifts
in the eaves are jumpy from lightning, leaving dry niches
till the long afternoon is full of arrowheads
    miraculously
never touching ground but only the rucked skirt of a
    pool.

Most days in downpour I'd picture a village-girl hiking
a bowled hip to bear a jerky bucket, her new teats
as hard as seagulls' heads, her full heart a bullfrog
in a waterhole of blood, and I imagine myself
hearty to her, a fellow she'd bring likely to a ditch
where I'd hit home and have my hour in her tiny cave
and kindle a flame with her, puff a claypipe after

and see the drear night out, Bridget whistling by the
    hearth.
Lately my wood of thinking is tree-tossed by despair
at ever outlasting the blights which creep upon me,
there is famine across the farm that is myself,
the blooms of good crops are blackening, my sweet will
sours in its well, the hill spring that fed me, Christ
and His field of lambs, has been changed from its old
    course

by some dirty cataclysm in the clay, a hurricane
or earthquake has passed through me as I slept. My wish
to live low and be Bridget's man as long as she allows
is a nut-tree that senses a boulder at its roots
or a beehive as a hedgehog knocks away the slate
or a mulberry banged by an axe. And dark as a cankered
    haw

I sit, and grip my blackthorn chair as if 'twere a
    terrible plough

or harrow to break the stale clods and mucky lakeland of
    a life.
It is here so by hard chance and a little grief that I
feel in my bones that the fairy is in my wife, and ask
    and ask
like a person at the door if she, black Bridget, be
    within
and take the doused lamp and the lamp-oil and move to
    rise
because only by trial of fire will I know, and now I cry
Oh by the Ark, the Temple and the Book, belovèd, are you
    there?

TROOPER O'HARA AT THE INDIAN WARS

My horse's head jangles on his martingale,
his spirit the same as this drenched May morning
with jewels of dew under the eucalyptus leaves
that rain on the ragworts, pearl before such swine.
My saddle is home
with a tuft of leather for my left hand
as our blue-coats brush through the mid-morning
and the red dust peppers the lather
and we are out among the Indian Wars.

Mulberries made the midnight of my hair
my mother said
which she knew from her berry gathering
to make her wine,
red, blue, goose, elder and sloe,
the lives of the blackthorn, my daddy's staff
in the cornmarket
through bins of the fading fool's gold of our farms
and the butter wharfs,
the sunk gold laced with salt to go to England.
My mother with her feet of many colours
after treading the oaken buckets
I think of, in the whey of here.

Yesterday, today, tomorrow
we kill wild native bowmen
savager surely than the English found us
I hope, or this is fratricide.
We burn out the girls in the tumbleweeds and brush
who lie quiet as turtles,
as soft as does of hares,
brothel and butcher-shop.

GIPSY CAMP, 1944

There are no large men with wings here,
no high paintings inside halls
of white figures with white wings.

The mothers' breasts are cut off
and photographs taken of the round wounds
leaving out the twisting faces.

I have seen even few devils,
old ones with grimacing mouths
and fishlike skins painted purple

or ones that squeeze out of churches
high up where the pigeons rest
under the copper angels.

But this is our enemy here,
the paintings and the wisps of music
that stray from the great buildings

when our journey brings us through.
Our journey. I remember the fiddle-tunes
moving between the tents like swifts

in the evening, with proportions
themselves of tents, the riffs,
and the engine-shy glooms of copses

and our silent familiar doors,
the soft flaps of March weather.
We lily'd the lay-bys with rags

so the settled wouldn't forget us.
If we had stayed less secret
or kept in the tigerish hills

and not shown our black faces
I wouldn't be tuning this pretend guitar
on my lap, with sores peeping through

like pennies, luck-money for horses.
Drizzle wouldn't be skirting
the towers, making the wire-fence

glisten like an injudicious web
and this camp wouldn't be without birds.
The hunger stops you going cuckoo.

If I let myself think of what happens
in the brick barns below the shelters
and the pall of smoke like a cloth

I wouldn't talk like this. They can
call us what they want but we were
something to envy. Look at our dances.

VOYAGE TO AZANIA
a letter to James Mathews of Athlone (Cape Town)

The deck is bedded with purple
blooms that wither or disappear
under the purser's footfalls.

The chairs were put out at
the start, and now the flying fish
match the queer colours

of the stripes. I am closeby
with a sandwich of lettuces
from the huge freezers. I met

an old dame in the dark
with a blackthorn stick, a moon
in her ear, waning or waxing

she could not say, or
I did not ask perhaps. She told
of her blanched sojourn in Switzerland

with a sculptor later famous
like Da Vinci maybe and how they crawled
into the hills together to ski

a long time ago when beer
was reasonable, and they lay
under the pineroof in the pinfall

darks in all their limbs
and made love like snowfall
and surface without a word

for fear of the couple next door.
But how they took to
the silence and the stealth

under the woollen roof! And
she thought that was all important,
to have a home, even a travelling

one. I thought of you and said
to the stars like small larks,
I must write to Jim

as I voyage on this vessel towards him
on a lost course no doubt,
through the scalloped expanse.

Old Europe I called her, old
missionary, tweed capes
and the trains on time, the first thing to go.

Would anything ever be
as normal as her again? The wind
monkeying in the mast-ropes, the bucket-hooks,

puts seasalt in the jam's glass bell
which I balance on my dusty
knees. All afternoon I searched

under the bunks for the blown
haystack, a bloom on some
subsistence farm, with the bees' luxury,

the muck on the milch-cow's tail
brushing and stirring
the brown planklight in the barn

but every wisp was gone. The real
birds in the gritty rigging
are out of picture-books, I knew

their names by the time I was five
but have forgotten them,
brushstrokes with soft wings resting briefly

on the cottony wood
till the notion or eternity
takes them, but whisks them where?

(I don't care about that anymore).
We trekked in the public park,
snuffing under the hand-warm

seats with the windy tramps
for the sootfalls, the sweepings
of the tribes from the municipal

brooms, the designs on the dark lawns
not local in the musk of the moon,
shelly as a bone spoon. The

birds, the woman, the fish, the bowl of ship!
I am glad I paid this passage
and left the crane-filled

shore. I see nothing but
the signalling of the fins
and shadows of words, any words.

FANNY HAWKE GOES TO THE MAINLAND
FOREVER

Ashblue porcelain, straw dolls, child's rocking-chair,
neat farms, boxwood beards, gilded sheaves for prayer,
Fanny Hawke of Sherkin Island, Quaker,
leaving her boundary stones to marry
a Catholic lithographer in Cork City,
no one on the new pier to wave her away,
neither an Easter visit or Market Day.
Only the hindview of a sleepy fox, its brush

shoving like a sheaf of sense through bushes.
Goodbye to the baskets in a judged heap
in an angle of the breakfast room,
the sun ignoring the Atlantic and leaping
alone into the midst of her family,
rustle, starch, and grave methods,
to that good hypocrisy, goodbye.
Goodbye little brother with your long face.

Small smooth shells on the great strands
come with her on her fingers as nails.
She smells the lobster the boatmen found
in the ghostly sea when she herself was asleep,
waiting while she dreamt for this morning,
something spangled and strewn on the lightly
grassed dunes, something tart in the air
while she walked, banging her skirts.

Come, little Fanny Hawke, into the bosom
of us hard Catholics, be an outlaw for us.
Bring what you own in a seabox on
a true voyage like anything worthwhile,
your linens with simplest stitchings,
your evening head-cloths, your confident
plainness. Be sure that you bring all fresh
despite that they have cast you completely

onto the desert and mainland of your love.
Up the century, Fanny, with you, never mind.
Look at your elegant son, an improved Catholic
squaring up landscapes in his future
to paint them as they are like a Quaker.
There is your other son, a scholarship painter,
a captain in a war, asthmatic, dying young,
all happening even as you set out, oh Fanny.

THE BACK OF THE SMALL FIELD

Turf lay in the seed,
"a necessity" the old man
stacked first in a design

we grew to admire
and stick to, loaves
for a holy show. One

morning in a dew
I found him, a flounder
alive on the flinty

threshold, with one
last breath to fog
his kingdom. Old fisher,

good-bye. Certainly
he brought me up
Knockboy on the bright

bike to wake those
trout, tumbling from tuft
to tuft in a muffle

of drizzle to the boggy
lake, the moon ashed
in the smoking. Fifty

hooks drifting, fifty
dreams. Then blindly
home, half wasp in the head

through the muddles
of the track, a longest way
metalled by brogues

and timely stones, with
"our bit of tea". O mice
on the rafters, pray for me.

THE GOOD NIGHT

"Throw in a few herbs,"
he whispers, a fur-splash
of cinders on his tea

and can't tell rosemary
from my good night
skimmed in the kitchen

between the dewy fiddle
the old man left
pressed like a fox

against the window-niche
and the scrubland of our
table darkening under

owls, my brother's lamp
of dandruff swung
against the rooty turf

speckling and spitting
under chimney drops
siphoning in

from an endless cold
like April's rats,
our straw and bolster

unfurling flannelette
above my strings of stiff
silver, "Josey, come to bed."

LINES DISCOVERED UNDER THE
FOUNDATIONS OF DUBLIN IN A LANGUAGE
NEITHER IRISH NOR ENGLISH
after a Medieval Latin song

These our winter quarters may
be heavyhanded under rain,
the shelters morninglike with grogblossom,

but we choose still
to stay on longer here
and spurn the citizens

who walk to give us walls.
O teenage men waking
to moony pleasure, throw

your perhaps ungrateful
words among our imaginary
stockades and make

your fathers witty
in case these townsmen
with charters and wardens manage

to bloom their kingship
in our babble and rubbish.
On disappearing

timber, tell our Echo
Mountain, not expecting
your maydays to boom back. O

berry men, aim to plumb
every available custom.
We can bear most error

for the sacred racket
of each of you roaring
to his melancholy

brother, "Keep the filthy
fathers inarticulate.
Keep nicks, companion!"

FIRST LETTER

Tree alphabets hold rights to praise
but what lost rights to exercise they are.
What alpha will address or dress her
to tell him too what he tells?

All lost in the telling then,
what they found in dumb-show
and knew as white on sight, a
sore-eye sight to who were dark.

Such linen, such paper, so typed
he was sure it could not be.
The white fool with his felicity.
A snow-blind snow-owl stumbling into her,

curled against linen. That is language,
hieroglyph, ogham, dead-sea scroll,
trusted to the dark by her manners,
unheard-of and not mistakable.

He turns in his lack to Alison.
All lost in the saying, and not alone.
Not heading back or tracking.
Astonished, dumbfounded, home.